Jackie AND Me

A VERY SPECIAL FRIENDSHIP

Written by
TANIA GROSSINGER

Illustrated by
CHARLES GEORGE ESPERANZA

Sky Pony Press
New York

Sky Pony Press books may be purchased in bulk at special dis-
counts for sales promotion, corporate gifts, fund-raising, or educational
purposes. Special editions can also be created to specifications. For
details, contact the Special Sales Department, Sky Pony Press,
307 West 36th Street, 11th Floor, New York, NY 10018 or
info@skyhorsepublishing.com.

Sky Pony® is a registered trademark of Skyhorse Publishing,
Inc.®, a Delaware corporation.

Visit our website at www.skyponypress.com.

10 9 8 7 6 5 4 3 2 1

Library of Congress Cataloging-in-Publication Data is available on
file.

ISBN: 978-1-62087-683-1

Manufactured in China, January 2013
This product conforms to CPSIA 2008

I was 13 years old when I met Jackie Robinson in 1951. He was the star of my favorite team, the Brooklyn Dodgers. In 1947, he became the first African American to play in Major League baseball. He was a hero to millions.

Many didn't like a black man playing in the Major Leagues. Jackie didn't care what they thought. He knew he could help the Dodgers win games, maybe even the World Series, and he wasn't going to let anyone tell him what he couldn't do.

Every kid I knew looked up to him. I did too.

Most people I knew grew up in a city or a suburb. Not me.

I grew up at a hotel as big as a castle called Grossinger's in New York's Catskill Mountains.

It was owned by my cousins, but they didn't always treat me like family and lots of times I felt like I didn't belong.

Lots of celebrities used to come to Grossinger's. They came to dance, eat, swim, and play tennis. Most didn't interest me at all.

The only celebrity I ever wanted to meet was Jackie Robinson, so you can imagine how excited I was the November day he arrived for a short vacation with his wife Rachel.

They even posed for a picture with my mother, but I was too shy to join them.

One afternoon, I stood in line with other girls waiting to meet Jackie. One girl was a champion speed skater. Another was a super skier. And then there was me, last in line as usual. What made me special?

As I approached, a man talking to Jackie said, "Tania plays a terrific game of ping-pong!" At that, a big smile appeared on Jackie's face.

"How about we play a game around four o'clock? Would you like to do that?"

Of course I said yes, but I didn't believe he really meant it.

Almost all the famous people I met promised things that didn't come true. So at four o'clock, I didn't show up. Instead, I went to my room that I shared with my mother and read.

Soon the telephone rang. It was Jackie Robinson!

"I thought we had a date," he said. "Did I make a mistake?"

Five minutes later I was in the ping-pong room. We played three games and had so much fun.

I cannot remember who won but it doesn't matter, because it was the happiest day of my life.

When we finished the last game, Jackie gave me a big hug!

When we sat down to have a soda, he asked me to explain why I hadn't come to meet him.

   "I didn't believe you," I said to him.

Jackie smiled and simply said, "Yes, dear. I think I do."

Years later I was embarrassed to have asked Jackie
that question, but I was just a girl then.

How could I have known that when Jackie joined the Dodgers, many people didn't want a black man to play baseball? He was taunted and yelled at often on the field.

After that day, Jackie and I started a friendship that lasted for years.

I would tell him how sad I felt because I didn't think I was pretty, and that my cousins picked on me because I was a very good student and they were jealous.

He told me not to pay attention to them, that I was pretty and should be proud that I was so smart.

"You should never be ashamed of who you are," he'd say. "That is what makes you special!"

One winter Jackie tried to learn to ice skate at Grossinger's. The first time he tried, he fell down. Then he fell down again, but he didn't care that everyone was staring. He just took a deep breath and tried again.

This time he put one foot
in front of the other
and was soon gliding
around the rink
like a pro.

"Never give up!" That's what he taught me.

A few years later, when I went to college, Jackie would write letters to me every time he came to Grossinger's, so that I wouldn't be homesick. I kept every single one. He'd often write: "I was so sorry you weren't here. We were looking forward to seeing you." Or: "We really missed you this time."

Whenever I felt lonely or
someone wasn't nice to me,
I would read Jackie's letters.
Knowing that he was my friend
made me feel very special.

I once told Jackie that when I turned 42 years old,
I would remember that 42 was the number he wore
on his uniform. And years later, the number 42 has
become the most important number in baseball.
Each year, on April 15—the day Jackie
first played with the Dodgers—every
baseball player on every team proudly
wears a 42 on his uniform. It
just proves how much he inspired
people all over, including me.

Jackie and I were friends for over twenty years, until he died in 1972. To America, Jackie Robinson will always be a hero. To me, he will always be my friend.